I Am Not a Wimp!

And, I'll Prove It!

FERNE PRESS

S0-AVF-249

By Julie Llewellyn ~ Illustrations by Jeff Covieo

This is a work of fiction. Names, characters, places, and incidents either are products of the author's imagination or are used fictitiously. Any resemblance to actual events, locales, or persons, living or dead, is entirely coincidental.

I Am Not a Wimp! And, I'll Prove It!

Copyright © 2012 by Julie Llewellyn
Illustrations by Jeff Covieo
Illustrations created with digital graphics
Layout and cover design Jacqueline L. Challiss Hill

Printed in Canada

All rights reserved. No part of this publication may be reproduced or transmitted in form by any means, electronic or mechanical, including photocopy, recording, or any other information storage and retrieval system, without permission in writing from the publisher.

Summary: A young girl is determined to learn to water ski during her family's summer vacation in Northern Michigan while proving to her older brother that she isn't a wimp.

Library of Congress Cataloging-in-Publication Data
    Llewellyn, Julie
    I Am Not a Wimp!/Julie Llewellyn—First Edition
    ISBN-13: 978-1-938326-00-4
    1. Juvenile fiction. 2. Water skiing. 3. Sisters and brothers.
    4. Family vacations. 5. Northern Michigan. 6. Summer activities.
    I. Llewellyn, Julie II. Title
    Library of Congress Control Number: 2012937418

FERNE PRESS

Ferne Press is an imprint of Nelson Publishing & Marketing
366 Welch Road, Northville, MI 48167
www.nelsonpublishingandmarketing.com
(248) 735-0418

Dedication

This book is dedicated to the memory of my mom, Noreen Ceuninck, who always encouraged me to do my best.

Acknowledgments

To my husband, Pete, who supported me throughout this process and made sure that he was home in time for me to get to writing class.

To my daughters, Brianna and Natalie, for showing me their enthusiasm for Mom becoming an author.

To my dad, Allan Ceuninck, without whom this entire story would not be possible.

Finally, to my family and friends for all their support and encouragement, especially my cousin, Peggy Bushon, for all of her excitement.

Chapter 1
Saturday

~~~~~~~~~~~~~~~~~~~~~~~~~~~~~~~~~~~

"Today I'm going to do it," Gwendolyn said as she woke up. The sun shone through her bedroom window and a warm breeze blew in. "Look at the bright blue sky and the clear blue water on Rose Lake. This is the summer that I'm going to do it because I'm now ten years old, double digits." She quickly got out of bed and put on her rainbow bathing suit.

After she was dressed, Gwendolyn raced to the kitchen.

"Good morning, Mom," she said. "What's for breakfast?"

"Good morning, Gwen. I can't believe that you're already awake even after getting here so late last night from Ann Arbor. Do you want cereal or scrambled eggs?"

"I'll have some eggs. Can I also have some juice and raspberries?"

"Sure," said Mom as she fixed breakfast.

"Do you know what today is, Mom? I'm going to water ski."

"Well, we'll be going on the boat right after breakfast and the kitchen is cleaned. I'm sure that you'll try your best to get up on skis. Remember to keep trying, and have fun."

Gwendolyn finished breakfast quickly, cleared her place at the table, and ran down the grassy path to the beach to wait for the rest of her family.

"Oh no, where's the boat? Where'd it go? Duh," she said, hitting herself on the side of the head. "I forgot that we need to clean it and then take it to the boat launch." She raced back across the sand and back up the grassy path to the shed behind their cottage to see if she could help get the boat ready. "The faster we clean the boat, the faster we can get it in the lake and I can water ski."

When she got to the boat, Dad and Phil, Gwendolyn's brother who was twelve, were already working on it. It was a small red, white, and blue striped speedboat with seats for six people in the back. There was also what Dad called the bow-rider in the front of the boat for four more people to sit in.

"It's about time you got here to help, Gwennie," said Phil. "What were you doing? Painting your nails?"

"Oh, be quiet, and don't call me Gwennie."

Ignoring her brother's questions, Gwendolyn asked Dad, "What can I do to help?"

"You can get a bucket of soap and water and a sponge and start cleaning the seats," said Dad.

"Boy, do these seats need to be cleaned. There's dirt and dried leaves stuck to them." Gwendolyn got the soapy water and began her cleaning project while Dad and Phil began checking out the motor. "And what is that smell? It smells like worms and wet leaves. Maybe dead and rotting worms."

"The spark plugs look fine and the gas hose seems to be intact. Let me go get some gas, and then we'll make sure it starts," said Dad.

"What do you mean you have to go get gas? Aren't we ever going on the boat?" asked Gwendolyn, putting her hands on her hips.

"We'll get the boat in the water after I get the gas and make sure the engine starts," responded Dad. "I'll be right back."

2

When Dad got back, he put the gas in the engine and put the motor in a bucket of water. "Okay, Phil, start it."

The boat started right away, but it was now time for lunch. Gwendolyn quickly ate her peanut butter and jelly sandwich and raced to get her blue and purple striped beach towel. Finally, the family got into the minivan and drove to the county park about ten minutes away to put the boat in the water.

"I can't believe I have to wait again," Gwendolyn announced when they got to the county park. There were two cars ahead of them in line to launch their boats. "This is going to take forever."

While they were waiting, Mom and Gwendolyn got out of the van and walked along the beach next to the boat ramp. Beach towels lined the sand, and people were running in and out of the water. Some were busy swimming while others relaxed on the shore. The roar of engines could be heard as seaplanes rose out of the water and others flew down to the lake. Seagulls walked along the beach in search of crumbs and bits of food, squawking as they went. On the far end of the beach, kids were playing on the swings and climbing the slide that went into the water.

Finally, it was their turn. Dad began to back up the trailer. Phil stood in the water and motioned for Dad to turn more to the right so that the trailer wheels would stay on the cement slabs in the water. If Dad drove too far to the right or left, the trailer could get stuck in the sand. Once the trailer was far enough in the water, Dad unhooked the boat. The boat floated in the lake, and Dad tied it to a pole on the shore. Then he moved the minivan and boat trailer back to the parking lot. When he came back, the whole family got into the boat and put on their life jackets, and Dad drove to the sandbar.

"I'll go first so you can see the perfect way to water ski, Gwennie," teased Phil.

"You can go first, but I'm sure you won't ski perfectly. You're not a pro, you know."

Turning his back on her, Phil tightened his red and orange life jacket, jumped into the water, and swam to the sandbar. "Here, Phil," said Dad, handing him the skis. "Be careful with these. Remember, they're old. They were the ones that your grandpa used and they're made of wood. I don't want them to crack."

"I know, Dad. I've used them for the past two years." Phil took the skis and leaned back to put them on, making sure that the tips of the skis were sticking out of the water. Then he grabbed the ski rope, put it between his skis, and gripped the handle.

Once the boat was directly in front of him and there was tension in the line, he yelled, "Ready!" Dad put the boat in gear and hit the gas. Phil glided to a standing position and began skiing.

"That looks easy," thought Gwendolyn as she sat in the bow-rider with the wind whipping her hair into her face. "Do you have a ponytail holder, Mom? I'm tired of eating my hair."

Mom handed her the tie as Phil continued to ski around the area by the sandbar.

"It's my turn!" yelled Gwendolyn. Phil kept skiing. Gwendolyn began motioning with her hand for Phil to stop. As the boat came around the sandbar again, Phil finally let go and glided into the shallow water.

"You've got a great day to water ski. The water is like glass—not a wave in sight," said Dad, pointing all around the five-mile-long lake. He turned the boat in a circle and headed back toward Phil.

"It's about time. How's the water?" Gwendolyn asked Phil as she tightened her pink life jacket.

4

"It's really warm."

Gwendolyn jumped into the lake and shivered. "Liar. It's not warm. This water is freezing." She swam quickly over to her brother.

"You know," said Phil, "you're only ten years old. I didn't get up on skis until I was eleven."

"Well, maybe I'm a fast learner."

Phil slid the bindings in the center of the skis to make them smaller for Gwendolyn and helped her put them on.

"These skis don't feel nearly as tight as I thought they would," she said.

"Here you go." He gave her the handle of the ski rope.

"Phil, don't forget her ski tips need to be up and out of the water," called Dad.

"Aw, Dad. Wouldn't it be fun if she fell face first into the lake?"

"No, it would not be. You need to help her learn to ski."

"Okay, fine."

Once her ski tips were in the right position, Phil held her under her arms to help her get up.

"Keep your legs straight with your knees slightly bent," Phil told her.

Gwendolyn gripped the bar-like handle tightly with both hands and yelled, "I'm ready!"

The boat moved slowly away from her. She didn't realize that she would be so far away from it. Gwendolyn was pulled by the boat, but as she started to stand she felt one of her skis falling off.

"Stop!" she yelled, but the boat kept moving. She screamed as she fell into the water and she had to let go of the rope. Mom looked worried as Dad turned the boat around and came back toward her.

"Gwen, are you okay?" Mom called out to her.

"You didn't get hurt, did you?"

"I'm fine, Mom. It did scare me a little, though, when Dad didn't hear me yell stop."

"I'm sorry, Gwendolyn. I'm glad that you're all right. Do you want to try again?"

"I sure do," she replied.

"You need to adjust the skis to fit Gwen's feet," Mom told Phil.

"What were you trying to do? Couldn't you tell they were too loose?" Phil asked, taking the skis from Gwendolyn to fix them. "You're such a dork."

"I'm not a dork. I thought that maybe I could go one ski like you want to do."

"It's called slalom skiing, and you need to get up on two first, Gwennie. Or maybe you should stick with tubing."

"I'm tired of sitting in that big inner tube being pulled through the water. I want more adventure," she said, putting her hands up in the air.

"Have it your way. Is that better?" Phil asked after he fixed Gwendolyn's skis and handed them back to her.

She put them on and said, "They feel tighter now."

She grasped the ski rope handle. "I'm all ready this time!" The boat moved forward and gained speed. "I'm standing!" she yelled as she continued to be pulled through the water. But then she looked down and realized she was only sitting. "This can't be right. Why can't I stand up?" she thought. Feeling frustrated, she finally let go of the rope.

"You have to stand up!" exclaimed Dad and Phil together.

"Boy, this is harder than I expected," she said to herself. "One more time!" she yelled to Dad, waving one finger in the air.

The boat moved forward, and she reached over to pass the long ski rope through her hands until she reached the handle.

"Hit it!" she yelled. As the boat lunged forward it pulled her up, but way too fast, and she fell face first into the water. She came to the surface coughing and gagging. She floated until the boat came back around.

"Are you all right?" asked Mom once Dad had circled the boat back toward her.

"I'm okay. I swallowed a lot of water," replied

Gwendolyn between coughs. "This isn't as easy as it looks. I'm done for today."

"Here you go," said Dad as he put the ladder down into the water so she could get into the boat. "You did a good job trying."

"Thanks, Dad. Maybe tomorrow I'll get up."

Chapter 2
Sunday

~~~~~~

"Yay!" exclaimed Gwendolyn when she awoke. "It's another sunny day. I'll wear this one," she said as she put on her blue and purple bathing suit. "It's my lucky suit."

She headed to the kitchen to find her family.

"Why are you all dressed up? Aren't we going on the boat today?"

"Did you forget that it's Sunday?" questioned Mom. "We're going to church this morning. We can go on the boat this afternoon."

"Oh, all right," she sighed. "I'll go change," she muttered as she slowly walked back to her room. "I need time to try to water ski."

"I'm ready to go," Gwendolyn announced as she came back into the kitchen wearing a sundress and sandals.

After breakfast was finished and the kitchen was cleaned, the family went to church.

"Amen," replied Gwendolyn at the end of the hour-long service. "Now we can go back to the cottage and I can go on the boat," she said to Mom. Just then, she felt a tap on her shoulder.

"Hi, Gwen. How are you?" asked Louise, Gwendolyn's up-north friend.

"Hi, Louise!" exclaimed Gwendolyn as the two girls hugged each other outside of church.

"Are you here all week?" asked Louise.

"Yes, we're here until next Saturday. What about

you?" she replied.

"That's so cool. Yay! We're staying until Saturday, too. Let's get together sometime this week."

"Okay, I'll ask my mom," said Gwendolyn. "Right now, we're going home to have lunch and then go on the boat. I'm trying to water ski."

"That's awesome. I just learned to ride on a knee-board. It was hard enough to pull myself up on my knees on a board. I can't imagine how hard it is to pull your whole body up and stand on two skis. Maybe I'll try skiing next summer. You'll have to tell me all about it."

Gwendolyn leaned over and whispered to her, "Later I'll have to tell you the real reason I want to water ski this summer. There are too many other people around now."

Louise started to say something but was interrupted by her mom calling, "Time to go, Louise."

As both families left, Gwendolyn asked, "Mom, when do you think I can get together with Louise?"

"It could probably be any day. We'll have to see what we're doing the rest of the week. Louise is probably staying at the same cottage she always does at the end of the road."

When they got home from church, Gwendolyn immediately went to put her bathing suit back on. Then she started to go outside to the dock, but Mom tapped her on the back, stopping her.

"Wait a minute, Gwen. We need to pack a lunch before we can leave. Can you help me get the sandwiches ready?"

Shrugging her shoulders, she replied, "How come I always have to make lunch? Where's Phil? Why can't he do it?"

"Your brother is getting the life jackets, towels, and skis into the boat."

"Okay," she said as she opened the refrigerator and got out the food. "I'll make the sandwiches then."

Together Gwendolyn and Mom packed lunch into a cooler and then walked down to the dock.

Once everything and everyone was on the boat, Dad tried to start the engine, but it wouldn't start.

"I wonder what the problem is?" he asked. He began to check the connections on the gearshift, but everything was fine. "I'll look at the motor."

When he got to the back of the boat, he lifted off the cover. "Okay, Phil, try to start it."

After Phil turned the key several times, Dad said, "Now I know what the problem is. The starter is broken."

"What's the starter, Dad?" Gwendolyn asked.

"The starter turns over, or starts, the engine. I'll have to go to the marina to get a new one."

"What's the marina?"

"You remember last year when we stopped at the store on the shore by the water? We got gas, some water to drink, and some fishing line. The place where the boats are docked outside the store is called a marina."

Gwendolyn nodded her head. "I remember that place. How long will it take to get the part?"

"The marina is right down the road, so I should be back in less than an hour."

"Well, hurry back, Dad." She ran down the beach and called over her shoulder, "I'll go swim in the lake while you're gone."

When Dad came back, Gwendolyn eagerly asked, "So did you get the part, Dad? Are we ready to go water skiing?"

"The marina wasn't open. It's Sunday and all the stores here in northern Michigan are closed. Norah is a small town, remember? We'll have to wait until tomorrow to get the part."

"What do you mean wait until tomorrow?" Gwendolyn stomped her feet a little. She felt her face get really hot.

"Don't worry, Gwendolyn. I'll get it fixed first thing in the morning," said Dad. "We'll spend today playing outside instead."

"Come on, Gwennie, I'll beat you in a game of croquet," said Phil.

"I'll win the game, and STOP calling me Gwennie," she called as Phil raced to the shed to get the croquet set.

"That boat better be fixed tomorrow or I don't know what I'm going to do," said Gwendolyn.

Chapter 3
Monday

~~~~~~

The soft tweeting of birds outside her window woke Gwendolyn. "Dad should be back from getting the starter for the boat. I'll wear my blue and purple bathing suit again today, since it is my lucky one. Today is the day that I will water ski," she said as she pointed her thumbs at herself energetically.

"What are you doing, Dad? Is the boat fixed already?" she asked quickly when she walked into the kitchen.

"No. The marina doesn't open until nine. It's only eight fifteen. I'll leave in a couple minutes."

"How long is it going to take to get to the marina and back? Remember I want to water ski today," she replied with her hands on her hips.

"Don't worry. You'll have plenty of time to try water skiing. The marina is about ten minutes away. I'll be there and back long before lunchtime."

"Before lunch?!"

"Relax. I was just teasing. I'll get back as soon as I can."

When he got back from the marina, Gwendolyn said, "Finally, you're back. Can we go on the boat now?"

"Well, I still have to put the part on and make sure that the boat starts. It shouldn't take long. Why don't you come help me fix it?"

Gwendolyn opened her mouth in surprise. "I've never fixed a boat before. Do you really want my help?"

"Yes, I think you should learn how to fix things. Go get your brother and meet me in the shed."

Gwendolyn raced through the cottage calling for Phil. She didn't get any answer from him. Finally, she spotted the closed bathroom door.

"Hurry, Phil. Dad needs us to work on the boat. What's taking you so long in the there?" she yelled as she pounded impatiently on the bathroom door.

Phil opened the door and brushed past Gwendolyn. He quickly headed outside and raced to find Dad. "What took you so long, Gwennie?" Phil asked when she got there.

The shed was a small white one-room building behind their cottage where all the extra life jackets, boat oars, and tools were stored.

"What is that smell?" Gwendolyn asked, holding her nose.

"That's the fresh smell of mothballs. It keeps the critters out of here," replied Dad. "Okay, I need a wrench, a socket set, and a Phillips-head screwdriver."

"What's a Phillips-head screwdriver?" asked Gwendolyn.

"Don't you know anything, Gwennie? It's the one with the X shape on the end. It's right there on the table."

Gwendolyn went over to the table and grabbed the tool. Then she began digging into the drawers in the old metal tool chest trying to find the rest of the things Dad needed. She held up dirty, brown, rusty instruments searching for the right ones.

"Is this a wrench?" she asked Dad.

"No, that's a socket wrench. A regular wrench looks like a letter C when it's opened."

"Here it is," she said, holding a filthy-looking wrench. She wiped the dirt off her hands onto her shorts.

Once all the tools were gathered, everyone headed down to the boat. Dad had docked it in front of the cottage.

"This is kind of fun, but it's taking a long time to fix," thought Gwendolyn as she handed tools back and forth to Dad.

Dad tightened another screw and then

announced, "Okay, let's see if it starts now." He turned the key in the ignition and the boat started to roar. "Well, it looks like it's ready to go."

"Hey, Dad, what's this stuff?" Gwendolyn asked as slimy black goop stuck to her hands.

"That's grease from the motor. Let's go back to the cottage to wash up."

As they walked into the cottage, Mom said, "I'll pack a lunch while you three grease monkeys get cleaned."

Once all the grease was washed off and lunch was packed, they all walked down to the boat. Dad drove the boat to the sandbar again because there was too much sticky, squishy muck in the water in front of the cottage to ski out from.

Gwendolyn and Phil jumped off the boat and into the water. "The water feels warmer today. I think this is a good sign that I'll ski."

"What are you talking about, Gwennie? Are you goofy?" Phil asked. "The water temperature has nothing to do with being able to ski or not. You have to be strong like me." He flexed his arm muscles.

"I have plenty of strength. I can do ten push-ups and two chin-ups," she said, pointing her finger at him.

"We'll see how much strength you've got. Here are the skis. The size should be fine since you used them last. Dad, throw us the rope, please."

Dad threw the rope. Phil grabbed it and handed it to Gwendolyn. As she clutched the small handle with both hands, Phil held her under the arms again to help her get up. She yelled, "Ready whenever you are!" to her parents in the boat.

The boat began to move forward and Gwendolyn felt herself being pulled too hard.

"Oh no," she thought and then splashed face

16

first into the water. She tried not to swallow any of the lake water but took some in anyway.

Dad circled the boat back toward her. She yelled, "I'll try again!" as she spit water out of her mouth.

"You can do it!" shouted Mom. "Keep trying, and hold your balance."

"You sure are strong," teased Phil as they waited for the rope.

"I'll show you how strong I am. Bring me that rope handle."

"Hit it!" she shouted to Dad. Again, the boat moved forward. "I can do this," she said, holding tightly to the handle. "Now if only I could stand up." She held on, crouching and being dragged through the water. But she couldn't get herself to stand up. Finally, she let go of the rope.

"One more try please, Dad," Gwendolyn begged as her father headed back toward her. "This time I'm going to make it," she told herself.

The boat circled around and the rope moved slowly past her. She leaned over to grab the handle. "Ready!"

As the boat moved forward, Gwendolyn felt her legs moving in opposite directions. She couldn't find the strength or the energy to push them back next to each other. Her legs did the splits and she fell again.

"Ow, my legs! They really hurt," she cried, tears forming. "I've had enough for today. My legs need a rest," she told her parents as the boat came back for her and Phil.

"You probably pulled the muscles in them. You're doing a great job trying," said Mom as Gwendolyn climbed back into the boat.

"I can't believe how hard it is to stand up on two pieces of wood and be pulled by a boat. Hopefully, my legs will feel better tomorrow." She began rubbing her sore legs.

Chapter 4
Tuesday

~~~~~~

"My legs are still a little sore, but I only have four more days of vacation," Gwendolyn said determinedly as she awoke in her still dark bedroom. "Oh no!" She looked out her window and saw a gray sky filled with clouds and rain pouring down. "It can't be raining! So much for water skiing today."

"Hi, Mom," she said sadly.

"Good morning, Gwen." Mom smiled widely. "What's wrong?"

"Is it going to rain all day? If it does, then I won't be able to try water skiing. It's so unfair!"

"Well, the weatherman said showers for the entire day with possible thunderstorms. Maybe you could get together with Louise."

She looked up at the sky as if a lightbulb had turned on in her head at that thought.

"That's a good idea. I'll go get dressed and then walk down to Louise's cottage."

She put on a pair of jeans, a T-shirt, and a rain jacket. "I really need boots to get through all this rain, but my old tennis shoes will have to do."

She ate a quick breakfast and headed out the door.

"Boy, this road really is wet and muddy," she commented as her shoes kept sticking in the mud. "I wish I was at Louise's already. I don't like walking through the woods when it's so dark and the trees are moving like that. I can't even see the sky. I feel like I'm in a tunnel." The cold rain fell steadily through the trees and pelted her on the back.

Suddenly, she was hit on the back by something bigger than a raindrop. "What was that?" she said. Then more small round balls came at her. She bent down and picked one up. "Those are blueberries," she yelled. "Who's out there?"

She slipped and fell on her bottom into the mud. As she pulled herself up, she heard a rustling sound in the trees and looked around feeling very afraid.

Phil came out from behind the trees laughing.

"You think you're so tough. You can't even walk through the woods without getting scared, Gwennie, and look, you landed yourself right in a mud pile. What a mess you are."

"Oh, why can't you just leave me alone? I was just fine walking through the woods until you came along to torment me. Go home and play one of your video games."

Then she turned and continued her walk to Louise's. She walked a little faster, though.

By the time she reached Louise's cottage, she was soaking wet, her shoes and clothes were caked with mud, and she was steaming mad at her brother.

"Gwendolyn, come right in. You're so wet. I'll go tell Louise that you're here," said Louise's mom.

"Thanks a lot. I don't think that I even get this wet when I'm swimming," Gwendolyn replied, shivering a little.

No sooner had Louise's mom left the room when Louise came running to greet Gwendolyn.

"Hi, Gwen. Let's go to my room and I'll get you some clean, dry clothes to wear. It's a good thing that you and I wear about the same size."

When they were in Louise's room, she said, "Here's a pair of jeans, a T-shirt, and a sweatshirt. You can go change in the bathroom."

"Thanks, I'll be right back."

As she came back into Louise's room, Gwendolyn announced, "That's much better. I'll be warm again in no time with your sweatshirt on."

"What do you want to do today? I guess we can't play outside. Maybe we could paint our nails. I brought some nail polish with me."

"That sounds great. What colors do you have?"

Louise walked over to her dresser and picked up the polish bottles. "I have one red, two pinks, and a purple shade."

"Let's use them all and make different patterns on our nails," suggested Gwendolyn.

As the girls sat on the floor and started painting their nails, Louise secretly asked, "Okay, what's the real reason you want to water ski? You were so mysterious on Sunday. I can't wait any longer to find out."

All of a sudden there was a flash of lightning. The lights flickered and went out. The girls screamed in a panic. Then, there was a boom of thunder, which shook the cottage windows. They slowly got up, keeping close to each other in the dark.

"I guess this makes things even more mysterious. I'll go get a flashlight or two from my mom. You can wait here, or you can come with me to find her."

"I'll come with you. I hate sitting in the dark during a storm."

As they left the room, a tree branch hit the bedroom window, making both girls jump, and they quickly raced to find Louise's mom.

With the light of the flashlights ahead of them, they went back to Louise's room to continue their conversation privately.

"Now, where were we? That's right, you were about to tell me the real reason that you want to water ski."

Gwendolyn began to paint her fingernails by the light of the flashlight. "You know how Phil is always teasing me. Today he hid in the woods while I walked here and threw blueberries to scare me. He brags all the time about all the stuff that he can do and what I can't. He tried to water ski when he was ten and didn't make it up until he was eleven. If I can learn to do it before he did, maybe he'd treat me more like how he treats his friends. Okay, he'll never treat me like that, but maybe he'd see that I'm not the wimpy girl or dork he thinks I am," she finished, putting her hands on her hips.

"Any luck, so far?"

"Well, I haven't made it up yet. I've tried two days this week and all I've done is drink a lot of lake water and get very sore legs. I really believe that I can do it."

Passing the purple polish back to Gwendolyn, Louise responded, "You're very brave. I don't think that I could keep trying. I got thrown off the inner tube once. It took me days before I would go back on. When I finally did, I only sat in it and let my dad pull me slowly."

Gwendolyn painted one nail red. "I know that if I don't keep trying, I'll never get up. I only have this week to do it, and I can't stand Phil always beating me. This is my chance to beat him at something. Maybe you can spend the night at my house tonight and then go on the boat with us tomorrow. You can be my personal cheerleader."

"That sounds terrific. I'm sure my mom will let me."

Chapter 5
Wednesday

~~~~~~

"When can we go on the boat?" Gwendolyn asked excitedly as she and Louise ran into the kitchen.

"You're both awake and ready to go?" Mom asked. "I didn't think that you would ever fall asleep last night. I can't remember the last time I heard so much whispering and laughing."

"Oh, we were only talking, Mom. Girl stuff, you know." The girls giggled.

After a quick breakfast, the girls raced outside to wait on the beach for the rest of the family.

"It's a good thing it's not raining today," said Gwendolyn as she looked at the clear blue sky. "There's not a gray cloud in sight."

"And it's starting to get hot, too. Looks like the perfect day for swimming and going on the boat," remarked Louise

"Let's build sandcastles while we wait," suggested Gwendolyn. She went over to a nearby tree and picked up the buckets that were on the ground beside it. Phil and Gwendolyn had left the buckets there after they returned from turtle hunting in the canal a few days before.

"What do we have here?" teased Phil. "Two bathing beauties?" Then he threw a bucket of water on the two girls.

"This is war!" screamed Gwendolyn as she grabbed a bucket and ran down to the lake to fill it.

"Well, who's ready...Wait a minute. What's going on here?" asked Dad as he walked down the path to the boat and got a face full of flying water from Gwendolyn's bucket.

"It's a water fight," responded Gwendolyn. "Phil started it."

"Did he?" called Dad as he got his own bucket of water and dumped it over Phil's head.

The group continued to race back and forth to the lake getting buckets of water to dump on each other.

"Take that, Phil!" yelled Gwendolyn throwing the water from a huge bucket on him.

"Oh, yeah? Here's one right back at you!"

"I'm here. Are we ready to go on the boat?" asked Mom as she approached the battle. She, too, got water all over herself.

Like Dad, she joined in the fun and ran to fill a bucket with lake water.

"Hey, Louise," called Gwendolyn. Once Louise turned around, she ended up with a face full of water.

"Some friend you are," laughed Louise, soaking Gwendolyn right back.

Once everyone was drenched, Gwendolyn remembered something. "Hey, aren't we going on the boat today?"

"Oh, that's why we're all down here," said Mom jokingly.

"Let's get some dry towels and then get on the boat," said Dad.

When they were all ready, Dad drove to the sandbar. Warm air blew through Gwendolyn's hair. She sat in the back of the boat with Louise and leaned over the side to put her hand in the cool water.

"Are you going to ski in this deep, dark water?" Louise asked.

"No, we start at the sandbar. The water isn't that deep there."

"Oh. That's good. It looks scary out here."

Phil and Gwendolyn jumped off the boat when they reached the shallow water.

"Boy, the water sure is colder today. All that rain yesterday must have cooled it down," shivered Gwendolyn.

"It looks cold to me, too," said Louise.

"Stop complaining and put the skis on. I'm getting tired of having to help you. You'll never get up anyway, Gwennie."

"Give me those skis. I'll show you."

She quickly put on the skis, making sure the straps were tight across her feet. Then she leaned over to get the ski rope handle. "Let him get a look at this. I can do it," she said to herself.

"Go, Gwen!" cheered Louise from the boat.

"Ready!" Gwendolyn called.

The boat moved forward and Gwendolyn felt herself being dragged behind it. She pulled herself up and out of the water.

"I'm doing it!"

She looked to the left to see another boat coming toward her.

"Oh no!" she exclaimed as she had turned her body too far. She let go of the handle.

The boat circled around as Gwendolyn bobbed up and down in the wake that was left behind by the two boats. She tried to keep her head above the waves, but it was tricky.

"Wow. Are you okay?" asked Louise as the boat passed Gwendolyn. "That didn't look too good."

"Did you see that boat? I thought it was going to

hit me!"

"The boat wasn't really close, plus I was turning to pull you in the other direction," replied Dad.

"Oh, stop all the yapping. She's fine," taunted Phil.

"I'm all right. Another try please, Dad."

Dad moved the boat forward so that the ski rope handle would come around to her. Gwendolyn leaned back, grabbed the handle, and bent her knees. "I'm all set!" she yelled.

She expected Dad to put the boat in gear and the boat to gain speed. Instead, it stopped.

"Now what? The boat better not be broken again."

"Don't worry," called Dad. "The boat is fine. It ran out of gas. I'll put on the extra gas tank and we'll be ready to go."

Once the new tank was on, Dad had to circle around again because the boat had drifted too far away from Gwendolyn.

The boat moved forward and Gwendolyn pulled the rope through her hands until she reached the handle. Again, she clutched the handle, leaned back, and bent her knees slightly. "Ready!" she called.

Gwendolyn felt herself moving forward and stood up.

"I'm up again," she said.

Then she saw that she was headed straight for a big wave. She struggled to hold her balance as she went over the wave. She teetered back and forth, but fell backwards with a huge splash.

"Ouch! My back!" she yelled, trying to keep her head above the waves as they came back toward her. She tried to adjust herself to reach her back and rub it, but couldn't with the waves and her life jacket.

She waited in pain for the boat to circle around.

"I'm done for today," she told Dad, waving her hand in the air. "It's your turn, Phil. One or two skis?"

"I'll use one," he said smugly.

"That sure looks hard, Gwen," said Louise once Gwendolyn was in the boat. "I don't know how you can keep trying to get up. It seems like a lot of work and no fun."

"My body is definitely getting a workout, but I can't quit yet," she replied, rubbing her back. "I'll rest and try again tomorrow. You were my good luck charm today. I actually got up two times!"

Meanwhile, Phil tried to get up on the one ski over and over again, but he couldn't do it. "I've had enough of trying to slalom for one day. Please put the ladder down so I can get into the boat," Phil muttered, shaking his head in disappointment.

"Dad, we're going on the boat tomorrow, right?" asked Gwendolyn.

"I believe that's the plan."

"That's great!" She smiled. "I think I'll make it up for sure tomorrow."

Chapter 6

Thursday

~~~~~~~~~~~~~~~~~~~~~~~~~~~~~~~~~~~~~~

"I'm all ready to go on the boat," Gwendolyn announced as she walked into the kitchen wearing her blue and purple bathing suit and carrying a rainbow towel.

"Oh, Gwen. Didn't I tell you? We're going to visit Aunt Gladys today," replied Mom.

"Do I have to go?" she stomped her foot and folded her arms across her chest in protest.

"Yes, you have to go. We always take one day to visit her when we're on vacation here. We'll be leaving in about a half an hour so we can be there in time for lunch."

"Fine. I'll go change."

Gwendolyn put on a sundress and sandals and came back into the kitchen. "I'm going to play on the beach. Call me when it's time to go, okay?" she said as she shuffled out of the cottage.

"What's wrong with you, Gwennie?" Phil ran up behind her from the woods. "Did you chip the polish off your nails?"

"No! We have to go to Aunt Gladys's today."

"I thought you liked going to Aunt Gladys's house."

"Well, I do, but we'll probably be there all day. At least I can have a fancy lunch and play with Barney. That crazy dog loves when I sing. He's like a funny little clown."

"Are you sure he's the one that's the clown?" Phil

teased.

"Time to go, kids," called Mom.

Once everyone was in the van, they started the drive to Aunt Gladys's. "How long is it going to take to get there?" Gwendolyn asked.

"Aunt Gladys lives in Jameston, which is about a half an hour to forty-five minutes away," replied Dad.

"I'm bored already," grumbled Gwendolyn.

"Oh, stop complaining, Gwennie. Why don't you read your book? I'm trying to play this game, and I can't concentrate with all of your talking."

"That's enough bickering, kids. Find something quiet to do. We'll be there soon," said Mom.

The sun was beating through the car windows and made Gwendolyn hot. She tried to read her book but couldn't focus and enjoy it. She knew that she shouldn't say anything, but she couldn't stand the heat any longer. "Dad, can you please turn on the air conditioner? I'm burning up."

"It's on full already."

Gwendolyn sat in silence staring out the window at the enormous tree trunks that passed by. As she looked way, way up, she could see the sunlight shining through the tops of the bright green trees. It was like driving through an enchanted forest, and she would have loved the scenery except that she had sweat beads forming all over her body. She could feel her legs sticking to the car seat.

"I hope that I don't stink and that it doesn't look like I peed my pants when I get out of the car," she thought to herself.

Finally, Dad turned off the road and they began to climb the steep hill through the trees to Aunt Gladys's house. As soon as Dad stopped the car, Aunt Gladys was at the front door waiting for them.

As they entered the house, they were greeted by

loud barking from Barney, Aunt Gladys's small brown and white dog.

"It's so good to see you," Aunt Gladys said, welcoming them. "Come right in. It's too hot out there today. Must be at least ninety degrees. Lunch will be ready in a few minutes. I hope you're all hungry."

Gwendolyn smiled at her aunt and began petting the dog at her aunt's feet. "Hi, Barney. How are you? Are you ready for a song?" Gwendolyn walked into the music room right next to the living room. There was a piano, drums, and her favorite instrument,

the ukulele. She plucked the strings singing,

"Barney Goo Goo, with the goo goo googly eyes.
He had a wife three times his size.

They got married then they got divorced.
Now he's sleeping with his horse.
Oh, Barney Goo Goo, with the goo goo googly
    eyes."

The dog ran and danced around to Gwendolyn's silly music.

"Time to eat," called Aunt Gladys from the kitchen.

"Sorry, old pal," Gwendolyn told the dog. "We'll have to continue later." She walked into the kitchen and asked, "What's for lunch?"

"We have chicken salad on croissants, fresh fruit salad, and lemonade. Can you go get one more special crystal glass, Gwendolyn? You remember where they are."

Gwendolyn got the delicate glass from the cupboard and brought it back to her aunt. Aunt Gladys filled it with lemonade for her. "What's the point of having these glasses if no one ever uses them? You can't take them with you," laughed Aunt Gladys.

"This is my favorite lunch. I feel like a queen." Gwendolyn giggled as she held the glass in the air with her pinky finger out like all the royalty do.

They all chuckled at Gwendolyn's acting.

"But I don't think a queen would have watermelon juice running down her chin, Gwennie," teased Phil.

"Maybe her servant looked away for a moment and forgot to wipe it for her," Gwendolyn replied.

"All right you two, we're going to have a pleasant lunch. Your aunt doesn't need to hear your bantering," said Mom.

"Oh, they're all right, my dear. That's how siblings are. I remember being teased by my older brother and then teasing my younger sister. No one ever got hurt, and we're still as close as ever today. Who's ready for dessert?"

Aunt Gladys served each of them homemade chocolate chip cookie ice cream sandwiches.

"Wow, these are so good," commented both kids.

"So what have you been doing this week?" asked Aunt Gladys.

"I've been trying to water ski, but I haven't been able to stay up," replied Gwendolyn.

"I remember learning to water ski, but I was fifteen before I could stay up."

"You skied?" both kids asked.

"Yes, I skied! How old do you think I am? I'm your grandpa's age, and he skied, didn't he?"

"Sorry, I was just surprised to hear that. Please go on with your story," Gwendolyn responded.

"Back when I was learning to ski, we had an old wooden boat. It had to be sanded, stained, and varnished each spring before we could even put it in the water. The work was hard, but we were lucky enough to even be able to afford a boat. When it came time to water ski, I tried and tried, but I couldn't keep my legs straight and hold my balance. Then my dad had a suggestion. He told me to keep my legs and skis closer together. Once he said that and I tried it, I was up in a flash."

"That's a good idea. I'll try it tomorrow."

"What about you, Phil? What have you been doing?"

Phil sighed. "I've been trying to one-ski or slalom."

"Oh, slalom skiing. My brother used to do that. It looked far too hard for me to want to try. He said that it was like walking on a tightrope or balance beam."

Phil slumped down in his seat, shaking his head. "I wouldn't know. I can't get up at all."

"Well, I'm sure that if you keep trying, you'll both be able to ski. My mother always said try and then try harder."

"That's great. I have one more day, and I think I'll take your advice," Gwendolyn said.

Chapter 7
Friday

~~~~~~

"I can't believe we're leaving tomorrow. This is the last day to water ski," said Gwendolyn as she rode in the boat with the spray from the lake hitting her face.

"Well, the sun is shining and the water is smooth as ice. It's not too windy, so there are no big waves to worry about," remarked Dad. "You have a perfect day to try skiing again."

They reached the sandbar, and the two kids jumped into the water.

"The water is warm, too," Gwendolyn said. "Hand me the skis please, Mom."

"Here you go. Good luck."

Gwendolyn leaned back and put the skis on. The boat had circled around, and she moved over to grab the ski rope handle as it came to her.

"Ready!" she yelled. "Legs together," she remembered as the boat moved forward.

She kept her legs together and she pulled herself to a standing position.

"I'm up! I'm really up!"

She looked around the lake and saw all the trees and the shoreline of beaches from her standing position. She couldn't believe the view she was getting. The feel of the wind through her hair was unbelievably great as she skied around and around.

"I can't believe it. I'm finally skiing. This is awesome. I made it. I reached my goal."

Dad circled around the area by the sandbar
a couple of times, and on the third time around,
Gwendolyn let go of the handle and glided up to the
sandbar.

"I did it!" Gwendolyn screamed. "I really did it!"

"That was wonderful," congratulated Dad as he
put the ladder into the water for Gwendolyn to climb
into the boat.

"Great job!" Mom exclaimed, hugging her wet
daughter.

"Can I go again?"

"No, your brother needs a turn," replied Dad.

"Okay, Phil, it's your turn," Gwendolyn said.

"Here, Gwennie. I'll only use one ski. Put the other
one away."

Phil tried to slalom three times but couldn't get
up. "I'm done," Phil said, shaking his head as the
boat circled back toward him. Phil got into the
boat.

Dad drove to the county park

where they were to meet Louise and her family for lunch.

"Louise, Louise. Guess what? I skied! I got up and stayed up! I went around and around!" she screamed, jumping up and down.

"That's great! Can I watch you?"

"Dad, can I ski again? Louise wants to watch me."

"We can go again after lunch, but remember we have to pull the boat out of the water today. We'll be leaving early tomorrow morning."

Gwendolyn and Louise ate their lunch between bursts of laughter.

"What's taking my dad so long? I want to show you how I can ski."

"Let's go, girls. Aren't you ready to go yet?" teased Dad.

Gwendolyn, Louise, Phil, and Dad got back on the boat, while the moms cleared the remaining lunch items.

"Phil, you can stay in the boat this time. I don't think that I'll need your help."

"Yeah, right. We'll see about that, Gwennie."

Gwendolyn jumped back into the water once Dad was at the sandbar. Phil handed her the skis. "Remember you have to tighten the binding on the one ski, since I used it last."

"Thanks, I'm not ready to slalom yet."

She fixed the size of the one ski and leaned back to put them both on.

Dad circled the boat around and she moved over to grab the handle. "Hit it!" she yelled.

The boat moved forward and Gwendolyn pulled herself to a standing position. She squinted as the sunlight glared off the water. "This is amazing! I can't believe that I'm skiing around the lake. This is so cool."

She skied around a couple of times and then let go of the handle as the boat rounded the sandbar. She glided into the shallow water.

"Wow, Gwen, that was great!" said Louise as Gwendolyn climbed back into the boat. "Maybe next year I'll be ready to try. You made it look so easy today."

"My turn," Phil interrupted. "One ski only, Gwennie."

Gwendolyn handed Phil the ski and turned back to talk to Louise.

"Thanks, Louise. We both know that it's not easy, but it sure is fun when you finally get up. It's like you're floating on air. Let's watch Phil."

Phil tried to get up on one ski, but he wasn't able to keep his balance and fell. As the boat came around again, Phil called, "I need the other ski."

Phil put the other ski on and was able to ski fine.

Dad drove the boat back toward the county park with Phil skiing behind it. As they reached the shallow water, Phil let go and glided in to the shore.

Dad tied the boat to a pole on the beach and had everyone get out. Then he went to get the minivan and trailer from the parking lot so he could take the boat out of the water.

Gwendolyn hugged Louise. "It was great seeing you. I'm so glad you were here to celebrate my water skiing with me."

"I'm so excited for you. I'll email you. Make sure you send me some pictures during the year."

"Definitely. Next year is your turn to ski. I'll be your coach."

"Awesome. See ya, Gwen."

"See ya, Louise." The two girls hugged each other goodbye.

***

That night once most of the stuff was packed, the family had a bonfire in the pit next to the cottage. The lightning bugs flickered in the night sky. Red sparks from the fire occasionally flew into the air.

"I'm so proud of you, Gwendolyn. You didn't get to try skiing every day, but you didn't give up," said Dad while moving out of the way of the campfire smoke.

"Thanks, Dad."

"I'm very proud of your determination, too, Gwen," said Mom. "I never did manage to get up on skis myself."

"Can you pass me another marshmallow, Gwendolyn?" asked Phil.

"What did you call me?" she asked, handing him a marshmallow.

"You heard me. You really surprised me. I don't like that you started skiing before I did, but that's really cool."

"I'm sorry that you didn't get to slalom ski. I know how it feels not to be able to do what you want."

"I think maybe I'll try Aunt Gladys's suggestion and practice walking on a balance beam. Of course, my friends back home can never find out. Right, Gwendolyn?"

"Mum's the word. But remember, you might have to try to slalom behind a horse next summer at a ranch."

Water Skiing Safety Tips

• ALWAYS wear a life jacket that fits properly and is approved by the U.S. Coast Guard.

• ALWAYS know the waterways where you will be skiing.

• ALWAYS ski and ride under control, at proper speeds, and within your skiing ability.

• ALWAYS have a capable observer in addition to the driver and agree on hand signals between the skier and the people in the boat before skiing.

• ALWAYS stay clear of engine exhaust to avoid carbon monoxide poisoning.

• ALWAYS turn ignition off when anyone is near watercraft power drive unit.

• ALWAYS read user's manual and inspect your equipment before using it.

• NEVER ski or ride near swimmers, shallow water, other boats, docks, pilings, or other obstacles.

• NEVER "Platform Drag" or touch the swim platform while the engine is running.

• NEVER operate a watercraft, ski, or ride under the influence of alcohol or drugs.

Adapted from the Water Sports Industry Association Watersports Responsibility Code.

Author Bio

Julie Llewellyn is the wife of Pete and the mother of two girls, Brianna and Natalie. They reside in Waterford, Michigan. Julie is the Girl Scout leader for both of her daughters' troops. In her spare time, she enjoys reading, swimming, building puzzles, and playing with her kids. For more information about Julie, please visit her at www.juliellewellynbooks.com.

Illustrator Bio

Jeff Covieo has been drawing since he could hold a pencil and hasn't stopped since. He has a BFA in photography from the Center for Creative Studies in Michigan and works in the commercial photography field, though drawing and illustration have been his avocation for years. Other titles illustrated by Jeff include *The Hero in Me, Cuddling Is Like Chocolate, Read to Me, Daddy! My First Football Book, Kyle and Kendra Go to Kindergarten, Logan and Lilly Go to Kindergarten,* and *The Ride of Your Life: Fighting Cancer with Attitude.*